allie
perea
marie
and allie
pereae
beet

For Johno,
every seven year old's expert on everything.

And special thanks to Elka, Bill Miller, Stephanie Thomas, Amy Sproull, Kathy Landwehr, and Mike Charles,
as well as to everyone who voted on the monsters, especially my friends at the MIT D.O.

— *K. S.*

To my family for the pencils, paintbrushes, and creepy stories.

— *M. A.*

All monsters portrayed in this book are real.
Any resemblance to imaginary monsters,
living or dead, is purely coincidental.

Published by PEACHTREE PUBLISHERS, LTD.
494 Armour Circle NE
Atlanta, Georgia 30324

Text © 1998 by Kevin Shortsleeve
Jacket and story illustrations © 1998 by Michael Austin

Jacket illustration by Michael Austin
Book design by Loraine M. Balcsik

Manufactured in Hong Kong
10 9 8 7 6 5 4 3 2 1
First Edition

Library of Congress Cataloging-in-Publication Data
Shortsleeve, Kevin.
    13 monsters who should be avoided / Kevin Shortsleeve ; illustrated by Michael
Austin. — lst ed.
        p. cm.
    Summary: Professor LeGrand introduces thirteen mischievous monsters, includ-
ing the Snit, Sissyfoo, and Thumple-haired Land Ant.
    ISBN 1-56145-146-0
    [1. Monsters—Fiction. 2. Stories in rhyme.] I. Austin, Michael, 1965-   ill.
II. Title.
PZ8.3.S55925Aaf   1998
[E]—dc21   97-11838
                                    CIP
                                    AC

13 Monsters Who Should Be Avoided

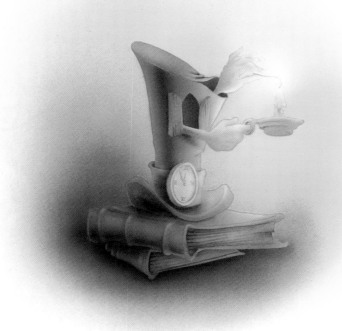

Kevin Shortsleeve

Illustrated by
Michael Austin

PEACHTREE
ATLANTA

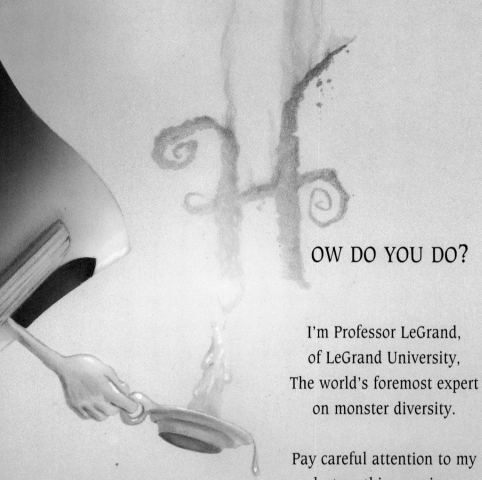

OW DO YOU DO?

I'm Professor LeGrand,
of LeGrand University,
The world's foremost expert
on monster diversity.

Pay careful attention to my
lecture this morning,
Take meticulous notes, and
remember this warning.

I have worked forty years on this neatly typed list
Of mischievous monsters whose natures consist
Of conduct I best can describe here at present
As something far less than what most would call pleasant.

Indeed,
Some monsters are charming; as guests they're enjoyed.
But the ones I'll describe are best to avoid.

Before we begin, I'll thank you for coming,
And request you refrain from all tapping or humming.

Now then...

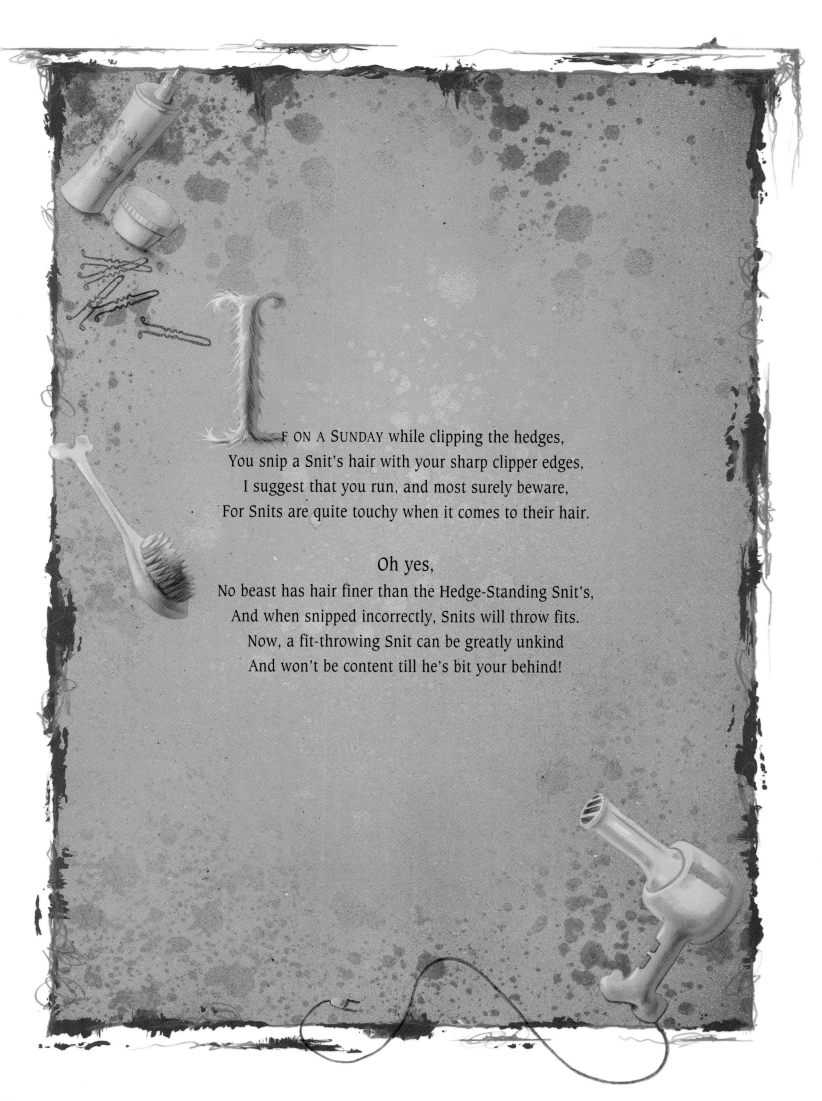

I<small>F ON A</small> S<small>UNDAY</small> while clipping the hedges,
You snip a Snit's hair with your sharp clipper edges,
I suggest that you run, and most surely beware,
For Snits are quite touchy when it comes to their hair.

Oh yes,
No beast has hair finer than the Hedge-Standing Snit's,
And when snipped incorrectly, Snits will throw fits.
Now, a fit-throwing Snit can be greatly unkind
And won't be content till he's bit your behind!

SOME OTHER ODD CREATURES that are seldomly seen
Are the scarce Sissyfoos (who, I warn you, are mean).
They live in dark wells by old country roads,
Where they dine on wet sneakers and unlucky toads.

They're hard to observe, down deep in a well,
But if there's one in there I'm sure you can tell.
For despite what the Sissyfoos might say or think,
The fact is, quite simply, Sissyfoos stink.

THE THUMPLE-HAIRED LAND ANTS, found only on Mars,
Present you no problem far off in the stars,
Unless, out of boredom (for Mars is quite bland),
They decide an excursion would be rather grand.

So they pack up their cameras and Frisbees and jammies,
Grab their third cousins and brothers and grammies,
Fly down to Earth and rent an RV,
Pull up at your door, and demand to have tea.

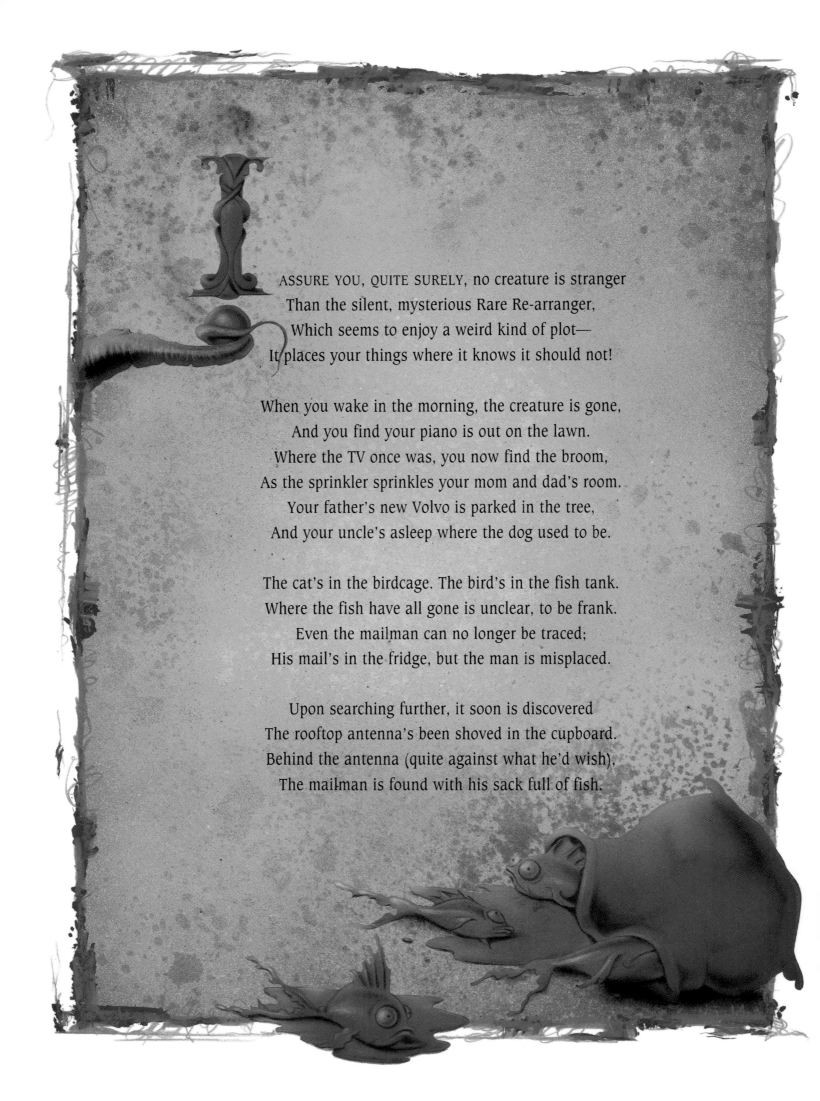

I ASSURE YOU, QUITE SURELY, no creature is stranger
Than the silent, mysterious Rare Re-arranger,
Which seems to enjoy a weird kind of plot—
It places your things where it knows it should not!

When you wake in the morning, the creature is gone,
And you find your piano is out on the lawn.
Where the TV once was, you now find the broom,
As the sprinkler sprinkles your mom and dad's room.
Your father's new Volvo is parked in the tree,
And your uncle's asleep where the dog used to be.

The cat's in the birdcage. The bird's in the fish tank.
Where the fish have all gone is unclear, to be frank.
Even the mailman can no longer be traced;
His mail's in the fridge, but the man is misplaced.

Upon searching further, it soon is discovered
The rooftop antenna's been shoved in the cupboard.
Behind the antenna (quite against what he'd wish),
The mailman is found with his sack full of fish.

T HE WHICHWAYAWAWA'S an utter annoyance.
For line-standing folks, he ruins enjoyance.
He buys tickets one-way by bus heading west,
And then decides two-ways due east would be best.

Then right when the "thank you" is leaving his mouth,
The Whichwayawawa decides to go south.
But just as the ticket due south is put forth,
The crazy thing panics and screams, "I meant north!"

This scene can go on for a very long time,
Making life rather grim for the next one in line.

If you're stuck behind him just tapping your toe,
Wondering which way the Wawa will go,
Don't worry, be patient—you're likely to find
At midnight he'll give up and say, "Never mind."

HREE MORE TO LOOK OUT FOR are Ralph, Ed, and Joe,
Who travel together wherever they go.
They share the same body and same point of view,
Which is, they'll eat anything, and that includes you!

But you might have a chance, since the trio is cursed
With three different views on what part to eat first.
Ralph prefers elbows and Joe likes the belly,
While Ed fancies toenails in fig-pickle jelly.

They never agree; they might argue all day,
Till finally they'll notice their lunch ran away!

'VE HEARD THAT THE CREATURE who's rarest of all,
The least well-known thing of the things who can crawl,
Only comes out when the moon is a sliver,
And the tide is half in on the Timbuktu River.

When the stars are in line and the wind's blowing east,
Then out slides the slithering Timbuktu Beast.
Yes, once every fifty-three years (so they think),
This creature creeps down to the river to drink.

Each time a crowd gathers to watch it appear,
And each time two tourists (or three) disappear.

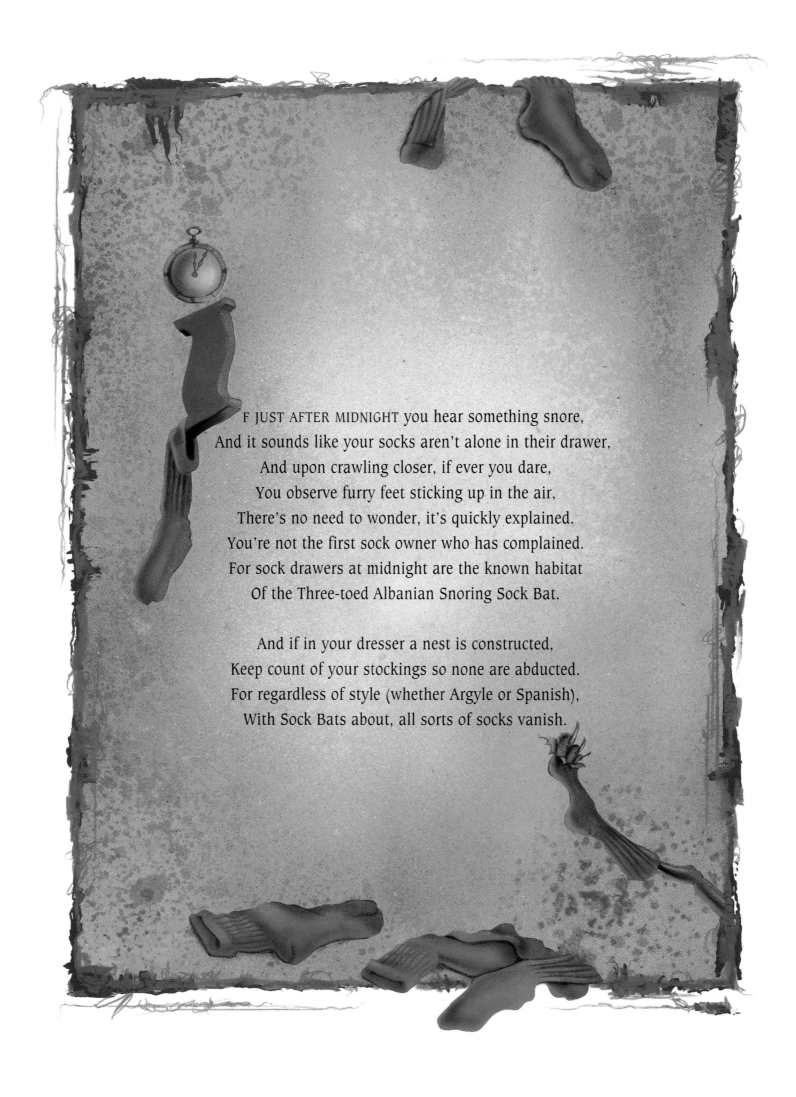

F JUST AFTER MIDNIGHT you hear something snore,
And it sounds like your socks aren't alone in their drawer,
And upon crawling closer, if ever you dare,
You observe furry feet sticking up in the air,
There's no need to wonder, it's quickly explained.
You're not the first sock owner who has complained.
For sock drawers at midnight are the known habitat
Of the Three-toed Albanian Snoring Sock Bat.

And if in your dresser a nest is constructed,
Keep count of your stockings so none are abducted.
For regardless of style (whether Argyle or Spanish),
With Sock Bats about, all sorts of socks vanish.

ESS MONSTERS, IN GENERAL, should not be let in,
Because once inside, Mess Monsters begin
To tip every lamp and spill every mug,
Tilt all the paintings and rumple each rug,

Topple the trash can down the front stairs,
Replace every lightbulb with sticky peeled pears,
Load the dishwasher with sport-fishing gear,
Drape soggy spaghetti from the brass chandelier,

Paint pudding-pie murals depicting a pig,
Stick bubble-gum wads in your aunt's silver wig,
Cut paper dolls out of your dinosaur poster,
And pour maple syrup right into the toaster.

Then the Mess Monster will suddenly shrug,
Say, "Sorry 'bout that," and give you a hug.
But before the Mess Monster can help you to clean,
He leaps on his scooter and flees from the scene!

ONE PROBLEM WITH SNURPS
from the Gamma-Goon Stars
Is their beastly behavior of eating parked cars.
Each one is a fiend and a dastardly plotter,
And each one has got his own giant car-swatter.

They hide outside theme parks and shopping-mall lots,
And swat helpless cars into nice chewy dots.
They gobble them up, then spit out the tires,
And pick at their teeth with the transmission wires.

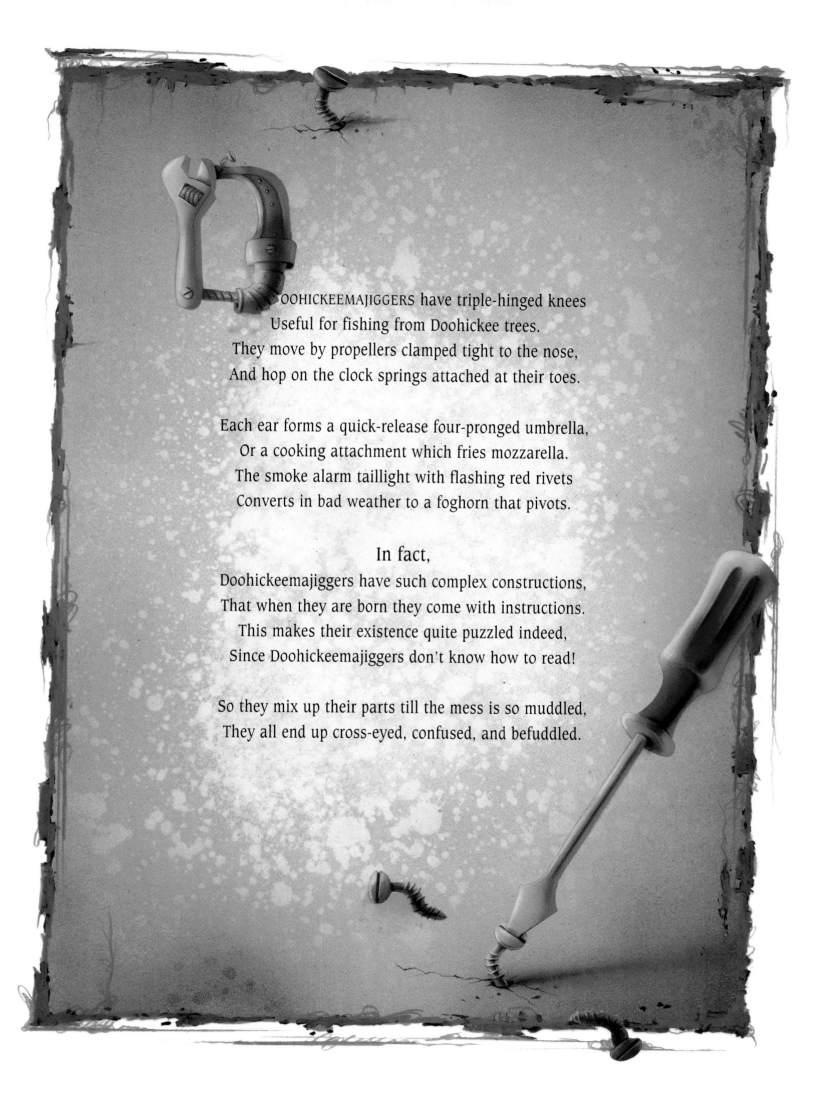

DOOHICKEEMAJIGGERS have triple-hinged knees
Useful for fishing from Doohickee trees.
They move by propellers clamped tight to the nose,
And hop on the clock springs attached at their toes.

Each ear forms a quick-release four-pronged umbrella,
Or a cooking attachment which fries mozzarella.
The smoke alarm taillight with flashing red rivets
Converts in bad weather to a foghorn that pivots.

In fact,
Doohickeemajiggers have such complex constructions,
That when they are born they come with instructions.
This makes their existence quite puzzled indeed,
Since Doohickeemajiggers don't know how to read!

So they mix up their parts till the mess is so muddled,
They all end up cross-eyed, confused, and befuddled.

ANOTHER ODD BEAST
whom I hope you don't meet
Is the thing with nine-hundred-and-ninety-nine feet,
Whose nine-hundred-ninety-nine rubber-soled sneakers
Are all rather new and the most horrid squeakers.

He likes to stop by for an unscheduled chat,
And wipe nine-hundred-ninety-nine feet on the mat.
If you do not have earplugs, I say acquire some,
For the squeaking involved here can be rather tiresome.

At Edward Van Akin's in Western Mercet,
Sits a thing in his room which is Edward's new pet.
It's a Gorg that he found in the neighborhood bog
(Who was hard to pull out of a half-submerged log).
He brought it straight home, gave it crackers and cheese,
Which it ate, with the plate, gulping down all of these.

When the crackers were gone, the Gorg ate a chair,
And then ate a towel, and then a stuffed bear.
Next came a ski boot, a decorative rug,
A football, a flashlight, and a jar with a bug.
Then it ate up the bed and the curtains and sheets,
And a very fine pair of bright green parakeets.

It slurped up Ed's homework and a Ping-Pong ball shooter,
Then down went his cd-rom four-meg computer.
It gobbled each book from off of each shelf.
Now all that is left is poor Edward himself.
Would a Gorg eat a boy? Should Edward beware?
Edward is sure that a Gorg wouldn't dare.

Unlucky Edward just might be mistaken.
I'm happy that I am not Edward Van Aikin.

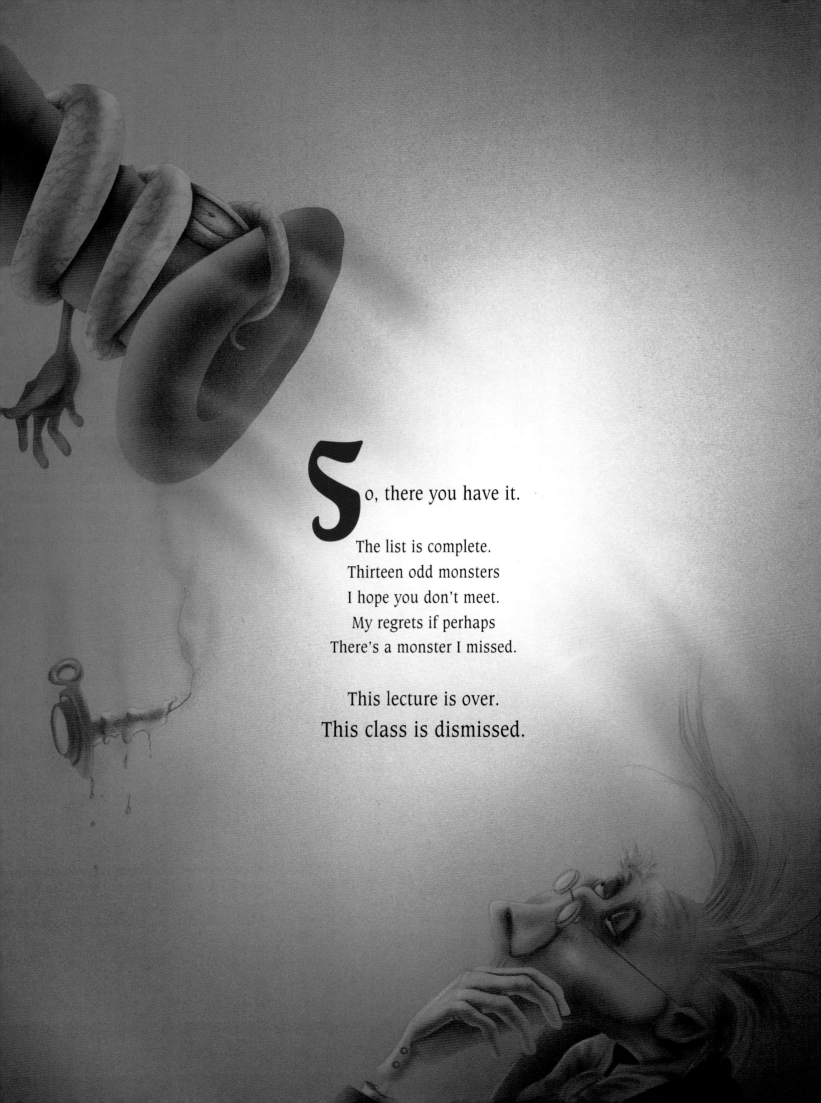

So, there you have it.

The list is complete.
Thirteen odd monsters
I hope you don't meet.
My regrets if perhaps
There's a monster I missed.

This lecture is over.
This class is dismissed.